My Treehouse

Written by Mary Roulston
Illustrated by Joy Dawood

Collins

Who and what is in this story?

Listen and say

Yusuf

treehouse

tree

Jill

Betty

garden

This is Betty's treehouse.
Betty wants to show her treehouse
to Yusuf and Jill.

Wow!
It's very big!

They go up the ladder to
the treehouse.

Betty says, "This is the living room."

Oh dear! Look at the cushion!

Betty says, "This is the kitchen."

Wow! I would like some food!

Betty gets some fruit.

Betty says, "This is the bedroom. These are my toys."

Oh dear. Look at teddy.

Yusuf says, "I like this!"
Betty says, "That's my doll's house."

Betty says, "My dolls live in the doll's house."

Betty says, "There are two bedrooms and a bathroom."

Jill says, "Look at this doll."
Yusuf says, "And this one!"

The children hear a noise.
Jill asks, "What's that noise?"

Betty says, "Let's go and look."

The children look in the garden.

They look up at the tree. They see a bird's nest.

Look! There's a family of birds in their nest!

Betty says, "It's my teddy's ear!
Thank you!"

Picture dictionary

Listen and repeat

bathroom

bedroom

cushion

doll's house

kitchen

ladder

living room

nest

1 Look and order the story

2 Listen and say

Collins

Published by Collins
An imprint of HarperCollins*Publishers*
Westerhill Road
Bishopbriggs
Glasgow
G64 2QT

HarperCollins*Publishers*
1st Floor, Watermarque Building
Ringsend Road
Dublin 4
Ireland

William Collins' dream of knowledge for all began with the publication of his first book in 1819.

A self-educated mill worker, he not only enriched millions of lives, but also founded a flourishing publishing house. Today, staying true to this spirit, Collins books are packed with inspiration, innovation and practical expertise. They place you at the centre of a world of possibility and give you exactly what you need to explore it.

© HarperCollins*Publishers* Limited 2020

10 9 8 7 6 5 4 3 2

ISBN 978-0-00-839716-6

Collins® and COBUILD® are registered trademarks of HarperCollins*Publishers* Limited

www.collins.co.uk/elt

British Library Cataloguing in Publication Data

A catalogue record for this publication is available from the British Library.

Author: Mary Roulston
Illustrator: Joy Dawood (Beehive)
Series editor: Rebecca Adlard
Publishing manager: Lisa Todd
Product managers: Jennifer Hall and Caroline Green
In-house editor: Alma Puts Keren
Project manager: Emily Hooton
Editor: Emma Wilkinson
Proofreaders: Natalie Murray and Michael Lamb
Cover designer: Kevin Robbins
Typesetter: 2Hoots Publishing Services Ltd
Audio produced by id audio, London
Reading guide author: Emma Wilkinson
Production controller: Rachel Weaver
Printed and bound by: GPS Group, Slovenia

MIX
Paper from responsible sources

FSC
www.fsc.org

FSC™ C007454

This book is produced from independently certified FSC™ paper to ensure responsible forest management.

For more information visit: **www.harpercollins.co.uk/green**

Download the audio for this book and a reading guide for parents and teachers at www.collins.co.uk/839716